Witch-in-Training
Training
Moonlight Mischief

D1390500

Cavan County Library
Withdrawn Stock

Other **Witch-in-Training** *titles*

Witch-in-Training

Training

Moonlight Mischief

Maeve Friel

Illustrated by Nathan Reed

HarperCollins *Children's Books*

CAVAN COUNTY LIBRARY
ACC No. C/201620
CLASS NO. J 5-8
INVOICE NO 7142 IES
PRICE €5·46

First published in Great Britain by HarperCollins *Children's Books* 2005
HarperCollins *Children's Books* is a division of HarperCollins*Publishers* Ltd
77-85 Fulham Palace Road, Hammersmith, London W6 8JB

The HarperCollins *Children's Books* website address is
www.harpercollinschildrensbooks.co.uk

2

Text © Maeve Friel 2005
Illustrations © Nathan Reed 2005

ISBN-13   978 0 00 718526 9
ISBN-10   0 00 718526 X

The author and illustrator assert the moral right
to be identified as author and illustrator of the work.

Printed and bound in England by
Clays Ltd, St Ives plc

Conditions of Sale
This book is sold subject to the condition
that it shall not, by way of trade or otherwise,
be lent, re-sold, hired out or otherwise circulated
without the publisher's prior consent in any form,
binding or cover other than that in which it is
published and without a similar condition
including this condition being imposed on the
subsequent purchaser.

CAVAN COUNTY LIBRARY

Chapter One

"Two dandelion clocks and a hair from the tail of a big red fox."

Jessica, witch-in-training, was busy mixing up a brew with her trainer, Miss Strega, at the hardware shop on the High Street when, out of the blue, there was a loud shout from the rooftop.

"Post!"

Jessica vaulted over the counter on her broom just as an envelope came fluttering down the chimney and came to rest on the shop floor.

"Goodness, this looks awfully important," she said.

At the top of the envelope there was a large black crest in the form of a spider web, surrounded by the words *Wishing the World Well*.

"It's a letter from Witches World Wide! And it's addressed to both of us. I wonder what they want."

Miss Strega stuck her wand behind her ear and took the envelope from Jessica. "I daresay they are looking for money – our annual fees or something," she said, as she slid a paperknife under the flap and drew out a stiff white card.

"Well, slap my tummy with a wet fish!" she gasped. "It's not a bill. It's an invitation."

"Yippee!" Jessica leaned over Miss Strega's shoulder. "Go on, read it out."

President Shar Pintake of the
Witches World Wide Association
is pleased to announce that
The Extraordinary Moonlight Games
will be held at our headquarters,
Coven Garden, to celebrate the
Blue Moon. Everyone is welcome.

"The Extraordinary Moonlight Games? What do they mean?"

"The Extraordinary Moonlight Games," Miss Strega explained, "is a special competition that only takes place if there is a blue moon in the seventh month of the witch year – and that doesn't happen very often. In fact I don't think there have been Moonlight Games for years and years. That's why they are Extraordinary."

Jessica looked baffled. "I don't understand a word you are saying. The moon is never blue when I vault over it with you. It's usually pearly-grey or white or sometimes yellow. Are you telling me that the moon is going to turn blue and that the witches are going to play games on it?"

"Actually, sugar plum, a blue moon is what we call the second full moon in a single calendar month. And the Games, as it says here, are held at Coven Garden."

"I see," said Jessica, nodding in what she hoped was a clever sort of way, although she was not quite sure that she had understood. "And what sort of Games are they? Do you mean playing cards or chess? Or do you mean games like football or tennis?"

Miss Strega cupped her long chin in one hand. "No, no, perish the thought; witches don't go in for that sort of stuff at all. It's more of a showcase for all the magic things

that we do – flying, spelling, switching, brewing, charming and chanting. There'll be everything from extreme sports like Synchronised Moon-Vaulting to individual Charming Demonstrations."

"Cool," said Jessica. "So I suppose there are competitions?"

"Precisely, my little tootle pip. There will be spectacular flying displays – watch out for the Ducking and Diving Fours – and, needless to say, there will be masses of Spelling and Brewing Competitions. Dr Krank won last time with a perfect Brew for Shrinking Bullies and your old friend, the actress Heckitty Darling, brought the house down with a stunning routine of Alphabetical Witch Switches. She switched from an ant to a zebra in twenty-six moves in less than a minute. I know she is a terrible show-off but you had to take your hat off to her."

"And are there prizes?"

"Are there prizes! Of course there are. For each event there's the Golden Broomstick, the Silver Cauldron and the Bronze Cat. Moonlight Champion Witches are celebrities, always popping up on television, getting their photos in the papers, hobnobbing with wizards and going to the best witch parties."

Jessica read the invitation again. "Perhaps," she said wistfully, "there are some events that witches-in-training can enter."

"Oh yes, indeedy," agreed Miss Strega. "The junior section is always fiercely contested. Are you going to take part?"

"I shall have a good think about it and then decide."

"Hunky-dory," said Miss Strega, propping the invitation on the mantelpiece, "but you had better make your mind up soon. You don't have much time for thinking."

"Why not?"

Miss Strega consulted a calendar on the wall. "Because the blue moon rises..." her index finger moved rapidly along the dates "...tonight!"

Chapter Two

Jessica perched on the chimneypot and watched the moon rise. It was one of the brightest moons that she had ever seen, like a giant party balloon that had lost its string and floated up into the sky. But the most peculiar thing about it was that, slowly but surely, it was turning bright blue.

Jessica blinked and blinked but, every time that she opened her eyes, there it was, bluer than ever.

"Come on," said Miss Strega, climbing through the attic window and clambering aboard her broom. "We must fly. We don't want to miss the opening ceremony."

The sky was very busy. Witches were streaming in from every direction – east, west, north and south and all points in between. Jessica had never seen so many – nor in so many different shapes and sizes and colours. There were huge giant witches with hooked noses and greasy, wide-brimmed hats; there were small twinkly witches with currant-bun faces; there were even some old-fashioned witches flying their broomsticks the Wrong-Way-Up. But best of all, she noticed excitedly, there were several other witches-in-training.

"Hi!" she yelled, taking both her hands off her control twigs to wave at them.

She was practically fizzing with excitement by the time the moonlit walls and roof turrets of Coven Garden came into view.

Jessica had often been to the witches' headquarters at Coven Garden before, even travelling back in time to see Dame Walpurga of the Blessed Warts, the witch who had invented the Modern Witch's Right-Way-Up Broom. In Dame Walpurga's time, Coven Garden was no more than a little cottage with a well and a hawthorn tree, but now it was enormous, like a walled city, bristling with towers and arched gateways. It had always seemed a bit scary-looking to Jessica (perhaps because she had had to take her Flying and Spelling Tests there too!), but tonight, in the light of the blue moon, it looked fantastic. She could hardly wait to descend on to the roof.

Unfortunately, there was only one narrow landing strip between the chimneypots, and the witches who were in charge of Flight Control were having a bad day.

So many broom riders were approaching the roof at the same time that there were long hold-ups. Everyone had to stack up on top of one another and circle around on their brooms until Flight Control called them down.

"Great honking goose feathers!" Miss Strega muttered impatiently. "If there is one thing I can't stand, it's queueing. If only we could find out how many witches are ahead of us."

"Hu-eet," whistled Jessica's mascot nightingale, Berkeley, her usual helpful self. She popped out of Jessica's cloak pocket in a cloud of biscuit crumbs and bird seed and sped off to find out what was going on.

When she returned a few minutes later, she was all a-flutter.

There had just been a very nasty crash, she told them. Some witch-in-training had got fed up waiting in line and had hurtled towards the rooftop

at the same time as another was landing. Boom! Crash! They collided at full speed, banging their heads and toppling off their brooms in a heap of legs and twigs and cloaks and helmets and squealing mascots.

"Come on, Jessica!" said Miss Strega. "Press your Emergency Descent twig! They may need help."

Sadly, by the time Miss Strega and Jessica had landed on the parapet, things had got much worse.

 The crashed witches-in-training had managed to disentangle themselves but they were now having a colossal row.

"You blinking road hog!" shrieked one of them, picking her scrunchie off the floor and gathering her long hair back into it.

"Call yourself a broom rider!" the second one spat back. "I've seen fish flying better than you."

Then, as Jessica and Miss Strega looked on, appalled but fascinated, the two witches-in-training started putting transformation spells on one another.

"You're no better than a spiky old hedgehog," screamed Ponytail.

"You're nothing but an old bat," the other cackled back.

"Moth!"

"Horsefly!"

"Pig!"

"Flying fish!"

And as if that weren't bad enough, they started putting spells on anyone who tried to stop them. And then *they* started putting spells on anyone who got in *their* way.

Soon, the roof was crawling with giant cockroaches and honking hogs, while monstrous moths and old bats and horseflies buzzed and flitted around the roof tiles. Miss Strega and Jessica quickly fled for cover behind a chimneypot and peeped around it.

"By Walpurga's Blessed Warts!" exclaimed Miss Strega. "What a lot of hocus pocus! All this – and the Games haven't even started."

"Who *are* those witches-in-training?" Jessica was flabbergasted. "They're a bit scary, but I wish I could spell as well as they can. They're lightning fast."

As she spoke, a very distinctive and blood-chilling sound brought everyone to their senses. It was the President of the W3, Miss Shar Pintake, noisily drawing in her breath and sucking her teeth as the doors of the glass lift slid open and she stepped on to the roof. She looked very presidential and imposing in her ceremonial dress – black velvet cape, tall witch's hat, turquoise and yellow stockings and a sash in the W3 colours of sage and purple – but she was clearly hopping mad.

All the witches hastily pulled themselves together.

"I have the Extraordinary Moonlight Games to judge tonight," Miss Pintake thundered. "I cannot allow this kind of broom rage to go on any longer. Surely it is not too much to expect the members of the W3 to follow simple instructions and make it into the building without all this kerfuffle."

"She started it!" shouted Ponytail.

"Oh no, I didn't. You barged in first!"

"Ariadne! Florinda! Enough!" Shar Pintake gave them both a withering stare.

She rummaged under her cloak and took out a long silver wand which she pointed at their heads.

"Time out!"

At once, the two witches-in-training were swooped up by the wind like a pair of

hooded crows and carried off to a traffic
roundabout in the middle of the roof.

Jessica's jaw dropped – Shar Pintake had
transformed them into a pair of stone
statues!

"Wow," she gasped. "Those poor girls. I wonder how long they will be stuck like that."

Miss Strega shook her head sadly. Then she gave a little giggle. "Their transformation spelling was a good laugh though, wasn't it? That's the great thing about being a witch – you can always get your own back if someone annoys you."

"Yes, but your opponents have lots of tricks up their sleeves too – not to mention the referee," Jessica added, as Shar Pintake sailed presidentially past the stone witches-in-training without a backward glance.

She thoughtfully chewed the end of her plait.

"Tell me, Miss Strega, do you think those witches-in-training will play fair and square at the Games or... do you think they might... I'm not saying they would cheat exactly, but... might they use secret spells or special potions or get up to other witch mischief?"

Miss Strega gave a little snort. "My dear little goose, witches will be witches. Come on, we'd better hurry. All the best seats will be gone."

Chapter Three

There was a complete crush in the central hall of Coven Garden when Jessica and Miss Strega finally managed to push their way in. The noise was deafening. Witches were cackling and screeching at the tops of their voices as they recognised old friends or foes. Their mascots were just as bad – cats were mewing (some of the more unfriendly ones were hissing), owls were hooting, frogs croaking and foxes barking. At the same time, loudspeakers pumped out famous witch tunes at ear-splitting volume.

At the far end, a number of celebrity witches were standing around a steaming cauldron having a brew. Some of them looked absolutely terrifying.

"They were the champions at the last Moonlight Games," Miss Strega explained, while Jessica stood on tiptoes to see them better over the moving sea of tall black hats.

Standing among the champions was a witch-in-training, sipping brew and cackling and smiling for the cameras. With her shiny cape and gleaming flying helmet, she almost glowed.

"Look," Jessica said, "who's that?"

"Oh that's Medea. She's the Moonlight Games Champion Witch-in-Training. She was hardly old enough to walk, let alone fly, when she won in the last Games. She's going to be some witch."

She looks very sparkly, Jessica thought. She was just about to ask if Medea was as bad-tempered as Florinda and Ariadne when the music stopped and the voice of Shar Pintake crackled over the loudspeaker.

"My fellow broom riders, please make your way at once to Dame Walpurga's Memorial Garden where I shall shortly be calling for the Grand Opening Witch Muster. Thank you."

"Chop chop," said Miss Strega, steering Jessica towards the arched door that led to the garden. "We want to get seats with a good view."

The garden looked quite different to the last time Jessica had been there. There were tiers of wooden seating around the walls, all of them already jam-packed with witches from every corner of the earth, and a high stage right in the centre of the garden near Dame Walpurga's Well (famous for its so-called magical water – Miss Strega even sold bottles of it in her shop). But she recognised at once the old hawthorn tree – she had once crash-landed into it when she was trying out an old-fashioned Wrong-Way-Up broom – and the statue of Dame Walpurga and all her Blessed Warts looked just the same.

As they shuffled past, some of the visitors to the Games made a great fuss of throwing a coin in the well for good luck; others touched the largest wart at the end of Dame Walpurga's nose and said a little chant. Others stopped to hang little ribbons or mini broomsticks or shoe buckles on the hawthorn tree.

Jessica wiggled her nose. "I don't know why they do that. It's so superstitious!"

"You can never be too careful when you

are in the company of witches," Miss Strega replied, and she gave Walpurga's nose a quick pat while Jessica looked around for two empty seats.

"It's full up," she said. "There are more witches here than you could shake a stick at."

"Absolutely!" agreed Miss Strega, pulling a wand out of her cape pocket.

At that very moment, two witches in the front row stood up.

"Oh goody! Look – those two are leaving." Jessica grabbed Miss Strega's elbow. "That was lucky, wasn't it?"

"No, luck had nothing to do with it," Miss Strega disagreed, as she tucked away her wand and sat down. "I just cast a spell on them so that they suddenly thought they ought to go to the bathroom. Which reminds me…"

She passed Jessica a small glass bottle. "You had better rub a few drops of this cream on your neck and ears."

"Is it perfume?" Jessica asked, sniffing the bottle doubtfully.

"No," Miss Strega lowered her voice to a whisper. "It's my own invention, Protection Cream. When you wear it nobody can put a jinx or spell on you. It's just a precaution; you never know what sort of tricks these witches might get up to."

"The same sort of tricks that you get up to, I suppose," Jessica whispered back, putting the stopper back on the bottle.

Suddenly there was a long drum roll which made everybody jump.

President Shar Pintake came zipping across the garden on her broom and dismounted on the stage.

"Arise, Broom Riders of the Skies!" pronounced Shar Pintake. "Arise for the Grand Witch Muster at the opening of these Extraordinary Moonlight Games to celebrate the night of the Blue Moon."

There was another drum roll. A bugle horn sounded.

Section by section, in a great Mexican wave, the witches rose until there were hundreds of them rising and falling and saluting Shar Pintake with their brooms held

aloft (twigs forward, of course). Then the loudspeakers crackled into life with the opening bars of the W3 Anthem. The witches again rose to their feet and, standing to attention, began to sing together.

"Ca-ca-ca-cackle! Ca-ca-ca-cackle!
Witches Worldwide are we!
Ca-ca-ca-cackle! Ca-ca-ca-cackle!
Witches Worldwide we'll be!
Forever brewing, constantly stewing
Our Magick somewhere near YOU!"

It was so brilliant it made Jessica's hair stand on end.

"All hail to the Witch Muster!" declared Shar Pintake. "May your brooms never let you down and may your spells be binding. I now declare the Games OPEN."

At that, there was a huge explosion of Chinese crackers. Hundreds of them went off, one after the other until the whole garden was cloaked in a dense cloud of smoke. The moon turned even bluer.

Then out from behind the smoke there came a flight of witches, twirling and swooping and spinning over Dame Walpurga's Memorial Garden.

"Broom Riders and Witches, I give you The Moonlight Games Champions!" announced a voice over the loudspeaker.

The crowd went wild. They whooped and

cheered. They stood up on their seats and held their mascots aloft. Some covens waved flags, others blew trumpets and let off firecrackers. One witch, draped in an orange sash, solemnly beat the cauldron that she wore slung around her neck like an enormous drum.

Jessica felt her heart pounding as the Moonlight Champions Zoomed over her head, trailing clouds of smoke.

"This is the best thing I have ever seen in my whole life!" she said, turning to Miss Strega and whispering softly.

"Huh! First timer!" said a voice above her.

Chapter Four

Jessica looked up.

Medea, the Champion Witch-in-Training, was hovering above her head.

"Hi," Jessica smiled. "My name is Jessica. I'm a witch-in-training too."

"I didn't think you were a mascot," said Medea. "Anyway, what are you doing here?"

Jessica's nose twitched angrily. "I'm here to watch the Games, like everybody else."

"Just to watch? You're too scared to compete, are you? Too much of a mouse?" She tapped her wand on Jessica's shoulder and laughed.

Jessica could feel her neck and ears tingle where she had dabbed Miss Strega's Protection Cream.

Medea suddenly frowned. "You are not turning into a mouse!"

"Charming as always, Medea!" said Miss Strega. "Of course Jessica is not turning into a mouse. She wouldn't fall for a cheap old spell like that. And of course she is here to compete. I wouldn't be surprised if she knocked you off your Moonlight Games Champion Witch-in-Training pedestal."

Medea's eyes flashed. "I don't think so!" she sneered, then cackled right in Jessica's face, before spinning off.

Jessica was gobsmacked.

"What did you say that for, about my knocking her off her pedestal?"

Miss Strega smiled sweetly. "Because, my enchanting little lamb's lettuce, I would expect nothing less of you."

"I don't even know what competitions there are for witches-in-training. It might be some kind of witchy subject I haven't even done yet."

"Why don't you pop along to the information desk and find out. I'll keep your seat."

Blooming Miss Strega, Jessica thought as she made her way back to the main building. *It's bad enough having to take part in these Games without having Medea out to get me.*

There was no one at reception but there was a notice taped to the counter.

Competitors for the Witch-in-Training Championship Hurdles may be asked to demonstrate their skills in any or all of the following: spelling, brewing, flying, charming and switching.

Well, at least I have tried all of those, thought Jessica, relieved. *A little bit anyway.*

The qualifying heat will take place in the library directly after the Witch Muster and the Opening of the Games. Previous winners qualify automatically.

"Blithering batwings!" Jessica whizzed over to the staircase. "I hope I'm in time."

There was a mean-looking library assistant at the door, handing out badges to competitors. "Fill in this name tag!" she barked. "And wait over there with the others!"

Jessica slipped in between two other witches-in-training on a long wooden bench. One had a long ponytail down to her waist. The other was so spiky she must have had a whole pot of gel in her hair. Ariadne and Florinda, the speedy spellers! The witches-in-training who had caused all the trouble on the roof!

"Hi," said Jessica, "I thought Shar Pintake had turned you to stone?"

"Yes," said Ariadne, with a toss of her ponytail, "but she came back and took the spell off us just before the Witch Muster. I was petrified! I thought I was going to miss the Games."

"Me too," said Florinda. "And it wasn't fair because I didn't start the fight."

"Oh yes, you did!" Ariadne retorted.

Florinda gave her a hard stare. "I did NOT."

"You're just a—"

"Oh, stop it!" said Jessica crossly.

She stroked her ears where she had put Miss Strega's Protection Cream. All she needed was for Florinda and Ariadne to fly off the handle and Shar Pintake would be sure to change them *all* into stone statues.

No one spoke for ages. The library clock ticked loudly.

"Have either of you met Medea?" Jessica asked, to break the silence. "She's the Champion Witch-in-Training – she tried to turn me into a mouse but—"

Out of the blue, Ariadne stood up and stamped her feet.

"Why are we waiting? Why doesn't somebody come and tell us what we have to DO?"

"Why don't you just wait your turn, for once?" Florinda sighed loudly.

I don't believe it! thought Jessica. *I haven't met another witch-in-training until today and then all three of them turn out to be nightmares. That Medea is so stuck up she thinks she's the cat's pyjamas , Florinda has a rotten temper and Ariadne is SO impatient. I shall have to be on full alert and not fall for any of their sneaky tricks.*

She carefully began to check that she had all her lucky charms and pins.

"Right, girls," said the library assistant, frostily. "It looks like nobody else is going to turn up so we might as well get on with it. The first thing I want you to do is a Witch Switch (NO live animals please). Imagine you are on a spying mission in a restaurant – what would be a good disguise? On your marks, go!"

Jessica instantly turned into a table lamp and switched herself on.

Chapter Five

"Well done!"

Miss Strega was thrilled when Jessica came back and told her she had passed the qualifying heat to enter the Witch-in-Training Championship Hurdles.

"There are only four of us," Jessica explained, "Ariadne and Florinda, who don't stop bickering, that dreadful Medea, who tried to turn me into a mouse, and me."

As she was speaking, the spectators burst into loud applause as the first witch in the Moon-Vaulting competition landed in the garden and flew over the finishing line.

"What exactly do you have to do?" Miss Strega shouted over the noise.

"It's a sort of race around the garden but with a lot of tasks along the way. First we have to fly backwards as fast as we can to a line of spell boxes, find the key to open the right box, read the spell that is inside, then rush to a cauldron, make up the correct brew and cast the spell. It's got something to do with rabbits."

"Sounds like lots of things could go

wrong." Miss Strega looked at her watch. "Perhaps I should make you a batch of Confusing Powder. It's marvellous stuff. You scatter it on the other girls' shoes and it really gets them into a muddle. They'll trip over themselves, fall off their brooms and generally forget where they're supposed to be going. Of course, you must be careful not to accidentally get any on yourself."

Jessica drew herself up to her full height. "Miss Strega, if you don't mind, I'm going to do this on my own."

"Would you not dab on some of my Protection Cream, at least? That little bit you put on earlier will have worn off by now."

"I've decided to play fair and square," said Jessica firmly.

Miss Strega stroked her very long chin. "Whatever you think best, gum drop," she replied.

"Witches and Crones!" the voice on the loudspeaker announced. "I am delighted to announce the commencement of the Moonlight Games Witch-in-Training Championship Hurdles. I'm sure we are in for a big treat. Will all the competitors please make their way to the starting line?"

Jessica Zoomed off.

*

The four witches-in-training lined up in their appointed lanes.

Race officials gave each of them special race helmets and racing numbers, which they wore over their capes, whilst Shar Pintake gravely inspected their brooms for any unapproved attachments.

Jessica was feeling really nervous as she fumbled with her helmet strap. She silently chanted, *"I can do it, I can do it, I can really do it."*

"...And they're under starters' orders," said the voice on the loudspeaker. "And they're OFF. It's Ariadne taking the lead on the straight as she approaches the first hurdle, with

Florinda and Medea neck-and-neck behind her. Jessica in the fourth lane seems to be struggling at the rear with broom problems."

Indeed, Jessica was finding flying backwards tough going. It was crazy. She was zigzagging all over the place as if her broom were being pulled sideways by a swarm of invisible goblins.

"Moonrays and marrowbones!" she shouted, tugging at the Fast Reverse twig. "Why will you not fly straight?"

The broom paid no attention.

"And now, as they come up to the Spell Box Hurdle, Medea seems to be gaining on Florinda and, yes, now she is overtaking

Ariadne too. What a champion this girl is. I'm sure you can all remember her star performance in the last Games. She is way out in front now, reversing at a gallop towards the spell boxes, with Florinda close behind, Ariadne now in third position and Jessica still far back in fourth place. But wait! It looks like plucky young Jessica has literally kicked her broom back into shape and is picking up speed. She's got a lot of work to do to catch up with Medea, I fear, who has already opened the box and is racing towards her cauldron with Florinda and Ariadne in hot pursuit.

"Oh no! More trouble for Jessica there. Dear, oh dear, oh dear. Jessica seems to have disappeared into a patch of fog. It's a real peasouper. I'm afraid I can't see her at all any longer."

Jessica could not believe what bad luck she was having, first with the wonky broom and then this thick blanket of fog appearing from nowhere and swallowing her up. She couldn't even see her twig controls. She blindly kept going backwards until she heard a loud thump and realised she had just crashed into the table and knocked the spell box to the ground. She scrabbled around

on the muddy grass, groping for the box and then fiddling with the key as she tried to find the keyhole. "Come on, come on!"

Finally, she managed to undo the lock, grabbed the spell paper – no time to read it – and sped off in the direction, she hoped, of her cauldron.

She emerged from the peasouper just in time to see Medea triumphantly punching the air and a long-eared rabbit loping off into the stands.

The crowd were on their feet, yelling, "Medea! Medea!"

Moments later, Florinda took second place.

Jessica's cheeks were blazing as she stirred and stirred and crissed and crossed her brew.

"And Ariadne has just drawn her rabbit out of her hat, so that puts her in third place," said the loudspeaker.

"Hu-eet," encouraged Berkeley, wiping Jessica's brow with her wing feather.

"Everyone will have flown home by the time I have finished this," Jessica fretted. "Miss Strega must be having kittens."

But in the end, the brew came right. Jessica intoned the spell. A peeved-looking rabbit hopped out of her hat, gave her a scornful look, as if it were saying "About time!" and scampered off.

Well, thought Jessica, *so much for knocking Medea off her pedestal!*

"Better late than never, I suppose," Medea shouted over her shoulder. "Did you lose your way? Forget how to steer a broom?"

Jessica's eyes narrowed.

"Medea!" she hissed. "You may think you're a star with all your swanky clothes and everybody saying you're the best – but I don't." And she stormed off.

A few minutes later, she was sitting, still fuming, drinking a cup of Calm Down Brew with Miss Strega.

"There, there," murmured Miss Strega, soothingly, "you can't win 'em all."

"All?!" Jessica spluttered. "I came last!"

"Well, I think you did very well – under the circumstances…"

"What do you mean?" said Jessica.

Miss Strega topped up both their cups before answering. "It just crossed my mind that that fog was a bit unnatural."

Jessica stared at Miss Strega, her mouth open wide. "You mean…"

Just then, the announcer's voice interrupted the Hags' Derby: "President Shar Pintake has announced an enquiry into the result of the Witch-in-Training Championship Hurdles. All contestants are requested to come immediately to the President's Chair."

Chapter Six

By the time Jessica had pushed her way back through the crowds into the garden, Shar Pintake had ascended the stage beside Walpurga's Well and was seated in a vast throne-like chair, sucking her teeth and looking as if she could happily bite someone's head off.

"Up here, Jessica!" she commanded grimly.

Jessica was so nervous she could hear her knees knocking. She awkwardly flew up on to the stage and shot a glance at her fellow witches-in-training. Medea was looking a little less sparkly; Ariadne was impatiently tapping her foot on the floor; Florinda was looking bored.

Every witch in the audience was all ears as President Shar Pintake began to speak.

"My fellow witches," she said, "I regret to tell you that eyebrows have been raised about the conduct of the Witch-in-Training Championship Hurdles. We are therefore holding a stewards' enquiry – this will take the form of the Sincerity Seed Test. It is clear that someone has been up to mischief!"

She sharply drew in her breath, took off her half-moon glasses and looked so witheringly at the four witches-in-training that they all shrank back in horror.

"Come forward one by one and take one of these." Shar Pintake held out a silver saucer on which lay four transparent red pomegranate seeds. "If anyone has been cheating, and I say "if" – this is an inquiry, not a public ducking – then the cheat will turn as scarlet as the skin of the pomegranate. Come on, girls, we haven't got all night."

One by one the witches-in-training chose a seed and bit it. It was as crisp as a water ice. They waited. Jessica, though she had nothing to be guilty about, felt as if she were being roasted alive.

Suddenly, the crowd gasped.

Jessica gasped.

Medea, the Champion Witch-in-Training, was turning bright bright red!

"It is just as I feared," said Shar Pintake. "Medea, I accuse you of bamboozling, of unprofessional sorcery, to wit, putting a spell on a competitor's broom and creating weather hazards in breach of the Witches

World Wide Rule Book (Moonlight Games Section). You are a disgrace to the good name of Witches World Wide. Pack up your belongings and then come and see me before the end of the Games at Walpurga's Well. The rest of you are free to enjoy the remainder of the Games until I decide what to do about this unfortunate incident. Do keep out of trouble until then."

Jessica was over the moon with happiness. She could hardly wait to get off the stage and find Miss Strega.

On the other hand, Medea now looked as if she had eaten a lemon. She glared at Shar Pintake as she flounced off the stage and hissed under her breath.

"Nobody treats me like this and gets away with it. I *am* a star!"

*

The Moonlight Games went on all night long. The Walpurga Wailers won the Chanting Competition as expected; there was a surprise result in the Poisonous Potion Event when several competitors had to withdraw with tummy upsets and a complete outsider took first place, and Heckitty Darling won the Switching Contest for the third Games in a row.

The final event was one of the highlights of the Moonlight Games. Teams of Fighting Gasps raced each other across the night sky on double-handled brooms rather like catamarans, dodging planets, slaloming around constellations and smashing into asteroids. All eyes were looking skyward when a flash of something red on Jessica's left distracted her. She turned around to see

Medea hovering on her broomstick beside the hawthorn tree. She was behaving very oddly, looking over her shoulder as if to check no one was watching her. Her lips moved as if she was speaking or maybe singing to herself. Jessica tiptoed closer.

Medea appeared to be clutching something in one hand and looking up at the crown of the tree which was festooned more than ever with offerings.

She raised her arms as if she were going to tie something to one of the branches, then turned around, leant over the wall of Walpurga's well, and spoke again. Then she quickly brought her broomstick around and Zoomed out of the garden.

Jessica nudged Miss Strega. "I have just seen Medea hanging something on the hawthorn tree. She's just as superstitious as all the silly old witches who leave offerings for Walpurga. As if Walpurga can save her from the wrath of Shar Pintake!"

As the last team of Fighting Gasps returned to Coven Garden, the blue moon had begun to sink. Fingers of pink light flickered on the horizon. It would soon be dawn. It was time for the prize-giving ceremony and the Farewell Muster.

Jessica stood in front of the grandstand with Florinda and Ariadne. If Shar Pintake disqualified Medea then it might just mean that Jessica could have third place and receive the Bronze Cat.

"Would President Pintake please make her way to the Grandstand?" the loudspeaker announced.

Two minutes later, the announcer appealed again. "Would President Pintake please contact one of the Games Stewards?"

Two minutes later, there was another appeal. "Would anyone who knows the whereabouts of President Shar Pintake please come forward?"

Jessica and Miss Strega looked at one another.

President Shar Pintake had gone missing!

Chapter Seven

News of Shar Pintake's disappearance flew around Coven Garden.

"Where can she be?" the witches asked one another.

"Who is going to call the Farewell Muster?"

"Who is going to give out the prizes?"

"We can't leave without saying goodbye to her," they all agreed, "even if she is a bossy old boot at times. It would be terribly bad manners."

"That's true," said Miss Strega, "but we can't hang around here much longer. The sun will be up soon."

Jessica stared at the hawthorn tree. She had a flashback of Medea hovering there before she Zoomed off.

She shouldered her way through the melee of witches and seized the microphone.

"Excuse me!" she shouted. "I think I know where Shar Pintake is! She's on the hawthorn tree!"

The entire assembly of Witches World Wide swivelled around and stared at the tree as if expecting to see Shar Pintake sitting atop its branches.

"Oh no, she isn't!" said Florinda and Ariadne together.

"Yes, she is!" insisted Jessica. "But she's invisible. I mean I saw Medea acting oddly earlier. I'm sure she has cast a spell on Miss Pintake to get her own back."

"What do you think she has been turned into?"

"I don't know," Jessica admitted. "I just think she is on the tree."

"Then, let's look for her," said Miss Strega. She turned on her heel and the whole witch muster rose up like a cloud of black crickets and followed her.

Everyone stared at the branches, at the little broomsticks, the tiny hats, the raggy bits of cape, the teensy cauldrons, the shoe buckles and all the other gifts that the witches had left, hoping that Dame

Walpurga would make their wishes come true.

"I'm not getting the scent of a spell," said one witch, sniffing. "Everything here seems to be what it is supposed to be."

Miss Strega too shook her long chin from side to side. "I'm not getting any whiff of Shar Pintakeness either, Jessica."

Jessica sighed. "Maybe I am wrong. But I did see Medea acting oddly. And I heard her threaten to get her own back on the president."

"I heard that too!" said Ariadne.

"Come on, then!" said Florinda. "Let's check out this hawthorn!"

The three witches-in-training immediately set about picking off all the witches' offerings, one by one, as if they were dismantling an overladen Christmas tree, and passed them to Miss Strega.

Miss Strega inspected each one. "No," she said, "no, and no, and not this one either."

Soon the ground around the tree was littered with offerings and the tree was bare – but there was still no sign of Shar Pintake.

Then Jessica had an idea.

"Can we have a bit of shush?" she asked. "A complete and absolute shush. No noise at all."

Her tone was so confident that everyone immediately fell silent. It was so quiet you could have heard a snail squeal.

But then, they heard it – the unmistakeable sound of Shar Pintake breathing, sharply drawing in her breath and crossly sucking her teeth.

"She's here!" said Jessica, Florinda and Ariadne together.

"She's definitely here!" chorused the grown-up witches.

"She's in the well!" cried Jessica. "That's it! Medea leant over the well before she Zoomed off. She must have thrown Shar Pintake in."

Chapter Eight

Shar Pintake came up in the third bucket. Medea had changed her into a tiny pottery doll, so Miss Strega had to make up a spell to change the W3 President back into herself.

Shar Pintake was terribly shaken at having been tricked by a mere witch-in-training, and doubly embarrassed that it was another witch-in-training who had rescued her. She could hardly wait for everyone to go away and leave her in peace.

She raced through the prize-giving at a gallop. In the Witch-in-Training Championship Hurdles, Florinda received the Golden Broomstick, Ariadne got the Silver Hat and Jessica was awarded third place "for completing the course despite being bombarded and bamboozled with illegal spells."

Jessica couldn't stop grinning as Shar Pintake pinned the Bronze Cat on her lapel.

"And finally," said Shar Pintake, loudly sucking her teeth. "Before I summon the Final Farewell Muster and we can take to the skies, I have one final prize to bestow, awarded by popular vote." She looked over her half-moon glasses and slit open the envelope that the steward passed to her.

"The Dame Walpurga Medal for this year's Extraordinary Witch of the Games goes to..."

The crowd waited.

"...Miss Jessica Diamond, witch-in-training!"

The witches went wild! They made a huge Mexican wave, waving their broomsticks above their heads and cheering: "Jessica! Jessica!"

Jessica beamed from ear to ear and bowed in all directions.

Miss Shar Pintake seized the chance to stumble off the stage and head for the lift.

Jessica caught up with her just as the doors opened.

"Madam President, please?" she said. "You know my trainer, Miss Strega – the one with the Witches' Supplies shop? Well, she has a fantastic new product – it's her own invention actually – Protection Cream, she calls it. A dab of that behind your ears every morning and you're a one-hundred per cent no-spell zone. You'd never have to worry about Medea or any sort of moonlight mischief again..."

She trailed off and turned a little red. "I mean I know you're perfectly good at protecting yourself, you're the president, but... Miss Strega's is on the High Street beside the toy shop."

Shar Pintake pursed her lips. She wasn't quite sure if Jessica was poking fun at her. Then she smiled. "Thank you, Jessica. Tell Miss Strega I shall look forward to visiting her shop."

As they left the bright lights of Coven Garden behind them and joined the stream of broom riders heading homewards, Miss Strega and Jessica passed a flight of unfamiliar witches with matted hair, hooked noses and tufts of long white whiskers sticking out of their ears like cats. But what really made them stand out was that they were flying their broomsticks the Wrong-Way-Up, twigs behind them, the way cross old-fashioned witches used to do before Dame Walpurga's marvellous invention.

Jessica was just about to pass them when she did a double take.

"Isn't that Medea down there with those witches flying Wrong-Way-Up brooms?"

Miss Strega looked down her long nose over the top of her glasses. There, spitting and fuming and looking murderous, was Medea, the ex-champion.

"By the screeching of Minerva's owl, I do believe you're right." She tut-tutted loudly.

"What a crowd of bad-tempered harpies. We should have suspected that Medea was the Wrong Sort of Witch. It's no wonder she's such a pain! Well, she shall drink as she brews. Shar Pintake will never allow her back to Coven Garden again."

"With any luck," added Jessica. "Come on, I'll race you to a Moon-Vault!"

CAVAN COUNTY LIBRARY

Witch-in-Training
Flying Lessons

Maeve Friel

Illustrated by Nathan Reed

On Jessica's tenth birthday she discovers that she is a witch! With Miss Strega as her teacher, and a broomstick to fly, Jessica is ready to begin her training. The first book in this magical series.

ISBN 0 00 713341 3

ROARING GOOD READS

Collins

An imprint of HarperCollinsPublishers

www.roaringgoodreads.co.uk

ENJOYED THIS BOOK? WHY NOT TRY OTHER GREAT TITLES BY THE AUTHOR – AT 10% OFF!

Buy great books direct from HarperCollins
at **10%** off recommended retail price.
FREE postage and packing in the UK.

- [ ] **Witch-in-Training: Flying Lessons** Maeve Friel 0-00-713341-3 £3.99
- [ ] **Witch-in-Training: Spelling Trouble** Maeve Friel 0-00-713342-1 £3.99
- [ ] **Witch-in-Training: Charming or What?** Maeve Friel 0-00-713343-X £3.99
- [ ] **Witch-in-Training: Brewing Up** Maeve Friel 0-00-713344-8 £3.99
- [ ] **Witch-in-Training: Broomstick Battles** Maeve Friel 0-00-718524-3 £3.99
- [ ] **Witch-in-Training: Witch Switch** Maeve Friel 0-00-718525-1 £3.99
- [ ] **Lilac Peabody and Sam Sparks** Annie Dalton 0-00-713771-0 £3.99
- [ ] **Lilac Peabody and Bella Bright** Annie Dalton 0-00-713772-9 £3.99
- [ ] **Lilac Peabody and Charlie Chase** Annie Dalton 0-00-713773-7 £3.99
- [ ] **Lilac Peabody and Honeysuckle Hope** Annie Dalton 0-00-713774-5 £3.99
- [ ] **Mister Skip** Michael Morpurgo 0-00-713474-6 £3.99
- [ ] **Pants on Fire** Victoria Lloyd 0-00-715525-5 £3.99

Total cost _____

10% discount _____

Final total _____

To purchase by Visa/Mastercard/Switch simply call
08707 871724 or fax on **08707 871725**

To pay by cheque, send a copy of this form with a cheque made payable to
'HarperCollins Publishers' to: Mail Order Dept. (Ref: BOB4),
HarperCollins Publishers, Westerhill Road, Bishopbriggs, G64 2QT,
making sure to include your full name, postal address and phone number.

From time to time HarperCollins may wish to use your personal data
to send you details of other HarperCollins publications and offers.
If you wish to receive information on other HarperCollins publications
and offers please tick this box [ ]

Do not send cash or currency. Prices correct at time of press.
Prices and availability are subject to change without notice.
Delivery overseas and to Ireland incurs a £2 per book postage and packing charge.